I0586843

A RABBIT'S JOURNEY

KODY B. NELSON

PUBLISHED BY

SIGMA'S
BOOKSHELF

MINNETONKA, MN 55305
WWW.SIGMASBOOKSHELF.COM

A Rabbit's Journey by Kody B. Nelson

Copyright © 2017 by Sigma's Bookshelf.

All rights reserved. No part of this book may be reproduced or transmitted in any form or by any means without written permission.

This is a work of fiction. Names, characters, places, and incidents either are the product of the author's imagination, or are used fictitiously. Any resemblance to actual persons, living or dead, business establishments, events, or locales is entirely coincidental.

Printed in the United States of America

Cover design by Sigma's Bookshelf using public domain imagery from Pixabay.com.

First Printing 2017

ISBN 978-0-9987-157-4-2

Dedication

To my bestfriend Corbs,
for inspiring this story to what it is now.

A Rabbit's Journey

It was the 13th century when it happened. My overly fluffy foot got caught in the time machine door, chopping it off completely and causing the hunters to think they were lucky to find the foot at all. In order to get my hopping abilities back to their maximum height again, I, Billford Fuzzies, would need to venture into the future to have a mechanic reforge a limb for me. With my friend Joey Darns, who is rather terrible at making friends other than myself for some reason, we headed into the mysterious future. We set the time core into overdrive to disintegrate any residue from the timeframe we were just in.

Now that the humans hadn't found their prey, but instead found another beast chewing upon what used to be one of my appendages, they probably thought finding a rabbit foot made them lucky. Well fat chance buddy!

That thing was EATING MY FREAKIN' FOOT! I knew the money it was gonna take to refill my health level was basically going to level my bank account once and for all. So much for carrots for every meal. Back to scrounging for potatoes and other sad vegetables. Carrots are the single most nutritional veggie in the world for any rabbit, and I myself am addicted to them.

Why did I go into the past you might ask? To find the

origin of the carrot and start a monopoly, that's why. If I was to gain control of the healthiest chunk of sustenance ever to grow out of this miserable dirt hole they call Earth, well, I'd be the richest rabbit in history. I'm already pretty rich actually. My family single-handedly invented and has an unlimited patent on the time machine industry. My true motivation for the carrot monopoly was actually to become even more famous.

As I stood one footed in the robotic limb section of the local parts store, waiting for the foot to be fitted with laser measurements, I began to ponder my situation. There always seems to be something standing in the way of my success. The only thing standing in my way of fame, however, is the slightly high chance that I may have schizophrenia. But Joey is the one thing keeping me confident. I am perfectly normal. I don't need friends like any average and platitude person. I AM A UNIQUE BUTTERFLY WHO WON'T BE CONTAINED BY THE CONFINES OF SOCIETY! And that, kiddos, is when my plan fell apart by the seams.

While still in the future, I was put into a mental hospital complex and was being examined by the top psychiatrists in the world of rabbits. In this time period, the once mighty human race had gone insane and animals ruled the world. The transition of power had happened after animals, frustrated with what was happening in the world, started talking to the humans and calling them out on their problems.

Humans couldn't fathom what was happening around them and lost it. Now they were more like a commodity, you know, creatures to laugh at because of their utter baseness and stupidity compared to us high and sophisticated animals, especially rabbits. But, anyway, back to the 21st century.

With my professional doctor captives looming over me, and judging my thought patterns as closely as a hawk would watch its nest to make sure the hatchlings don't throw any killer parties without them, I, the great Billford Fuzzies, felt like such a troglodyte. I was secluded in this yellow, plush room with the dust settling on my excessively tight straight jacket after every slight movement that I reluctantly decided to take. The worst part of this, however, is that for some reason Joey, the Darns fool, got to roam about the compound and laugh at my predicament through the glass watch bay from where the doctors continue to pile on diagnostics and medication to my already extended list of stuff I'm required to take.

I was just about to make my daring escape when they suddenly let me out. They told me that I was cured as long as I took the meds they gave me every day. However, as relieving as this was, I soon noticed that Joey, the fickle fool, was still inside the complex. Me, being the schizophrenic and amazingly good friend I am, simply had to go and save him! The rage that overcame me was almost beastly. So, in rage mode, I began to furiously plan a breakout.

Remembering that Joey loved watching the doctors watch me, I wondered if he could possibly still be in there. I decided that they MUST be holding him in the observation deck in the psychiatric ward. Forcing him to watch doctors, whilst they vigorously watch a poor and defenseless psycho. Unlike myself of course. That was just a misunderstanding.

After a long night of convoluting and scheming, I had my action plan ready to be put to the test. There was nothing those dorks could throw at me that I couldn't counter.

The next morning, soon after dawn, I began the heist. I didn't get very far before encountering my first problem. The doors were locked. After pushing and shoving with all my might, they still did not open to my calls for entry. Almost ready to call it quits right there, I frustratingly tried to weigh the odds that I could just go on without Joey.

I mean he was never really of much help anyway.

Then in a Godlike stroke of luck, the doors opened. A doctor (in a trick I will never understand) just yanked the door open as if it wasn't locked at all! Some people are just wizards with these things. As I sneakily sprinted through the nearly closed door, I thought I saw something on the edge of insanity. A doctor and his patient LAUGHING? What had they done to that poor bunny? In this place of hellish proportions, how could there be anything close to happiness?

Avoiding the infectious toxins they must have been using, I ran past and found the room I sought. As I stepped into the white polished marble room, I suddenly noticed the doctors observing their current subject, a small black and white kitten, who seemed to be shaking violently when they played the sound of an accursed vacuum cleaner.

Back to the mission. In the corner next to the monitoring equipment, I saw Joey strapped onto an upright table, like the freak from a movie by the humans called Frankenstein. Joey started struggling rather loudly, so I rushed towards him as quietly and stealthily as I could. Before I could make it to him, he began screaming so loudly it amazed me that no one heard and raised an alarm. As I finally stalked up next to him, I felt a slight pain to my head, and he disappeared! I felt as if something in my life had left, and I could see clearly. But the loss I felt at this moment was too great to comprehend. My best friend had turned into smoke right in front of my eyes.

But WAIT! The TIME MACHINE! It was my only hope. I suddenly realized I could go back and save him from himself and his terrible one time habit of disappearing into mist. At the time, I just hoped I could get back before my father noticed that I had taken his favorite time machine. If he figured it out, I would be in trouble!

Without regard for subtlety, I worriedly made my way out of the complex, and rushed to the bushes where my time machine was expertly concealed. I saw a bunch of small bunny children circling the time machine like it was some kind of wondrous thing to find sitting in the bushes. I guess to them it was. Time machines must not be something you see every day in this town. I cleared a path to the machine while being assaulted with a wide barrage of questions about who I was from the curious children. More importantly to them, however, was the question of if I'd consent to taking them with me to see the world before they even existed.

Without paying them any mind I clicked the opener and stepped inside. With an inkling of a plan forming in my mind on how to get Joey back, I set the time modulator to the date I knew for sure Joey was there. The date I met him.

Now this isn't the typical story of friendship. No, it is the story of how a trillionaire playbunny came into contact with someone so interesting that they simply must become friends. The date we first met was actually in the year of the beginning. I had decided to go and witness the Big Bang bring everything into the known and unknown universe. While gazing hopelessly at the sheer size and awesomeness of this world creating spectacle, there he was, a lone human floating about. The only reason that I talked to him was to ask him if he thought there could ever be any more important moment in the entire history of all history. He wittily stated, "Of course there is. The moment that destroys all of this will bring everything to its knees with loss and regret."

And to that I replied, "Well, isn't that a bit of a negative outlook on our entire existence?" And like SNAP! We were instant comrades.

As I punched in the exact coordinates of our first encounter with life and everything, I sat in nostalgia of all the memories I've shared with Joey. Like the first time we went to my mansion, him gawking at all of its magnificent splendor, and proceeding to tell me it needs to have a chocolate milk dispenser for all of my numerous friends. The first time that I let him drive my Hop Rod 1500, and the sound of him freaking out when he couldn't handle it, lost control and went into the ditch of the universe, Mars. And then our last and most precious memory, the day he told me he would be by my side forever, always have my back, and would never let me go through life without achieving my goals. TRUE friendship is wanting the best for said friend and pushing them into becoming the best version of themselves that could ever be possible.

Having thought through all of these enriching memories, I begin to focus on the task at paw, physically saving Joey from the ball of nonexistent dust that he shall become in the extremely far away, yet closer than ever future. As the time machine slowed its timely descent into the target time zone, I got my gear ready so that I was able to withstand the Big Bang in all of its creative glory. This gear, which consisted of overly heavy and compact condensers of matter, would protect me from nearly anything (except a black hole of inescapable life draining proportions). As long as there's no black hole, all should go smoothly.

The time warp had been interrupted, so I knew that I'd arrived at precisely the right time. I finished putting on the final touches, checked the safety precautions to the suit, and prepared to jettison myself—with the keys—into the vacuum of nothingness which would soon be known as the universe. I awaited the timer and made a final inspection of my suit's oxygen levels, then suddenly and expectedly I was launched into the void where I hoped to find my friend and bring him back for dinner.

Blackness, pure darkness, all but a miniature orb of light. Not even the time machine could cast any light in this amount of darkness. Oxygen, ninety-five percent. I must have had a loose cable somewhere. It didn't matter. I'd only be here a minute or two, just enough time to find Joey. As I diligently searched everywhere in the dark with my keen rabbit night vision, a slight popping sound reverberated through my helmet as the universe was brought into existence. Oxygen seventy-two percent. I had to keep looking. Suit integrity levels, eighty-six percent. As many system warning signs popped up on my HUD, I ignored them and anxiously continued my search. After a few minutes passed, I received a notification. Oxygen levels reaching critical, twenty-three percent; suit integrity level, forty-eight percent; mental instability detected; and operator stress levels reaching questionably high amounts. Immediate action recommended.

I had to keep going! Joey would have done the same if it were me. I CANNOT JUST LEAVE I thought! And at that very moment I spotted Joey. Without a proper space suit like mine, he wouldn't last much more than five minutes in the current amount of radiation that had just been released. He began being pulled in by the time machine's tractor beam when suddenly, and rather ironically, a black hole spawned from where the orb of creation was just mere minutes before. As I put my thrusters into full overdrive, I silently sped like a bullet towards Joey to help in his perilous situation. I grabbed hold of his suit and pushed the thrusters into maximum hyperdrive. But it was just not fast enough. No light can escape a black hole's gravitational pull, and none ever will, as theorized by the great physicists of the human race before their downfall. In a fury, my plan was formulated.

If we could somehow get the time machine in between us and the black hole, we could open the launch bay doors, cut the thrust, and fall into the time machine; then try something that has never before been attempted before due to its potentially dangerous outcome. We were going to travel through time, through a black hole, which would hopefully slingshot us into the time that we wanted, perhaps the location as well. Well, here goes nothing I thought! We maneuvered the time machine into position remotely, and with pure luck and no mathematical calculation, we were able to hit our target and fall into the time machine launch bay. Next came the difficult part, getting the time warp to engage just before we entered the singularity and were slingshotted into a random place, time, or just plain obliterated.

I quickly and haphazardly discarded the smoking remnants of my space suit and sent a medical drone to attend to Joey, then hopped with all my speed to the central time control room. I prepped the warp drive, entered a random meaningless time frame, and set the coordinates which should put us near the outskirts of Mars, should we need a barren landing zone to crash in. The coordinates processed and began to spin through the map, deciding where to put the particles in the correct order so that we didn't end up as a random assortment of debris floating towards the backwards civilizations built on the ditch of the universe. As this happened, the event horizon pulled us closer towards the singularity, and its gaping maw of the unknown, other newly formed planets, speeding past towards their doom.

I carefully maneuvered my way around the incoming debris of mixed comets, smoldering planets, and asteroids of all sizes. If even one of a reasonable size was to hit the ship and change its current velocity, we'd plummet to almost certain death at the hands of a time wave explosion. Joey, in a seemingly drunken stupor, stumbled into the room and I noticed I had forgotten to turn on the ship's artificial gravity. I hit the controls for the time warp machine, changing the coordinates to somewhere roughly around the moons of Jupiter, closest to Titan.

This slight distraction might have ended us, if I hadn't just turned on the Warp Drive, which does the processes extremely quick, but at the risk of reassembling in the wrong order. At this point I figured, what could possibly make this situation worse than it already is? The Drive activated just as we reached the singularity, and... BOOOM!

We exploded back into existence. We weren't anywhere near the coordinates entered though, which was just out of Titan's gravity field.

I opened the star map on the console, and it gave a message stating, "No known constellations detected. Please relocate and or contact the number given below with your error code. Good luck!"

As the message finished, the power to the time machine cut out and we began to spiral towards a nearby planet, which appeared to be somewhat similar to Earth. As we hurtled towards the unknown planet, we felt chills as if some aetherial being had entered our bodies. The flames burst around the time machine as we entered the planet's atmosphere and crashed through some rather tall and strange trees. As our descent began to reach its end, we leveled a few structures which ended up flattening several of this planet's lifeforms. Knowing that this wouldn't end well, I prepped physical enhancement suits for me and Joey, so we could make a break for it if we got caught in a pickle with local law enforcement. Once the time machine stopped at the base of a tall treelike structure, we prepared to be swarmed by the local life, but to our surprise there was no one there.

As we stepped out of the launch bay doors, I heard a sound similar to that of rustling leaves off to the left of the doors. I felt as if there were eyes watching from nearly every direction, my every move being harshly scrutinized and analyzed. I got ready to run. Then Joey placed his hand upon my head. I looked up at him. He shook his head and said, "Everything's gonna be all right. They're peaceful I think."

Then I heard a voice calling in the distance, behind some foliage. "Billford?"

"Who's there?" I yelled back.

I heard the word, "SON!" and suddenly a bunch of my family members came hopping out of the bushes. In an instant I was swarmed by all of my relatives and strangers alike. They all wanted to know where I had been and what I had done. I answered the barrage of queries that were thrown my direction, and suddenly wondered where Joey had gone. I heard a sudden outcry to my right.

"HELP ME BILLFORD!"

It was Joey! He was being dragged away by some of the rabbit citizens!

"What's going on here?" I asked everyone, expecting my father to answer.

"These humans, they threaten our way of life! They revolted against our superiority the day after you disappeared, and there's been war between us ever since! It's been at least a few years since that awful day!"

I could not even fathom this statement. A FEW YEARS?!

"We were only gone for a few hours or days, according to the calculations on the time machine," I said to my father distraught and confusedly. Then I realized the gravity of the situation that we were currently involved in.

Even with Joey bumping into the time warp drive, we couldn't have gone into a different time, just a different location. Could the black hole have transported us through the space time continuum as well as through space? Or even worse, could we have been teleported into a parallel universe?! A universe where the bunnies were dictating overlords over the humans, and humankind revolted against them? This just isn't right! And why is it that suddenly my family can see Joey? During my time in the mental institution the doctors never seemed to take notice of Joey prancing around in the background, touching the equipment, and reading their notes. Now that I think about it... Did I take any of the medications prescribed to me by those doctors after being released?

"I'VE GOT IT!" I shouted loudly, "You guys don't remember Joey because Joey never existed before today! He was a figment of my diseased brain, made up to be a real person in my head, but my head alone!" This realization made me feel like sudden roadkill that was ambiguously run over by big rig trucks. Most of the adventures I experienced—they didn't even exist?! In my brain it made sense, following Joey through thick and thin, but on the outside, I must have seemed like a crazed lunatic, talking to air.

However, what in the world made Joey real? If he was just an imaginary figure, there is no logical way that he could just materialize out of thin air by the power of my brain... I'm not that smart. Then, another epiphany hit me. As we hurdled towards the planet's surface, I felt as if something aetherial passed through me, stopped at my brain for a moment, and then left, having taken something with it. Could Joey have manifested by this extra-dimensional being passing through my mind, and taking form? Is Joey still the same friend I used to know, or is he just a physical manifestation of this... Spirit? Half mumbling to myself, I said, "If this isn't our universe, we aren't in the right dimension. How do we get home?"

Well, at this point it didn't matter. We needed to get back home as soon as possible. Back to our original dimension, and our original lives.

Over all of the commotion of me returning, and Joey

being scrutinized for his race, I formed a plan to return to our proper dimension. "Dad, are you still working on a black hole traversing time machine? One that is meant to predict the potential outcomes of entering the singularity of the black hole?" My father looked at me with a baffled look, as if this invention were secret, but everyone in our family was involved with the time machine building process.

"No son. I stopped research for that when the war started between us and the humans. But, if what you seem to be saying is true, if this truly isn't the dimension that you originated from, you need to return to your real dimension as soon as possible. Otherwise our universe will tear itself apart by the seams because there cannot be two of the same beings in the same universe. The human's multiverse theory doesn't allow for more than one exact copy of any being alive in that universe at the same time. Thus the universe compensates for that when we time travel by making alternate timelines, keeping the present constant, and the time continuum from ripping itself apart, as it soon will if you stay."

"Then how do we get back? If what you're saying is true, we should only have a matter of hours, or even minutes!" I worriedly asked him.

He responded in the calmest and most fatherly voice I have ever heard. "Don't worry son, I think I can come up with a plan or two." All the while a big grin started to appear on his face. "Follow me if you want to live to see your home again!"

He took us into his laboratory, where the vines and other wildlife had taken root and were taking over the highly advanced rabbit technology lying around on the once white pearlescent flooring. "Over here!"

He pointed toward what was clearly an early prototype of one of his big ideas that could change the world. You know, that type of invention. However, this thing doesn't even look remotely close to finished, or even wired up and upholstered. I mean, what is this, the Bronze Age? We absolutely need to have the highest quality of hardwood or vinyl flooring, and pure alpaca leather seating, with inlaid golden thread and diamond studs on the back.

"It's a bit rough around the edges, but it might just suit your needs for interdimensional travel. I just need to finish wiring it up. We don't have time to run any tests on it. It's either die in a cool test to define a critical moment in science, or die by the universe locating you and snuffing you out."

"I think I'll take the second option please," I said sadly, as I wondered at the chances that this would actually work. "I'd rather die a quick and painless death by universal disturbance than die an infinite amount of times in infinite universes, all of which could be different and painful."

My father gazed at me with a look of disappointment and regret. "Stop thinking about how you're gonna die and start pondering how you'll live afterwards. Either way, this is your only chance. Now, come over here and help me wire this thing up son."

I made my way over to where my father had restarted his old project, lining up the wires to be connected, checking the fuel lines for any radioactive leakage, and then finally beginning to put some high contrast LEDs into the control panel, for aesthetic purposes. Just then, a sudden and violent tremor of planetary size washed over the area in a wave of cosmic power.

"There's just no time! Hurry up and help me with this!" I started to hop on over towards my father when I noticed that my head was spinning, and my body felt light and faded. The void loomed over my head. It seemed as if the time had come for me to leave this world, when suddenly my father and Joey yelled and began to pull me out of my mesmerized state. "The universe has found you! We need to leave now!" Joey stated to the entire room of nothingness.

"I agree. The only thing that kept you here was our reality conflicting with yours. So, as long as we are real, we force your molecular structure to remain in this dimension, but we must remain in physical contact. The universe won't destroy one of us just to get at you, but it will soon find a way to bypass our reality and take you away."

He hobbled back over to the dimensional traversing machine, and plugged in the last few wires to the control panel. "There! everything should be in order! Joey, help Billford get inside. I'll enter the coordinates and run the setup programs. I just need a sample of Billford's fur in order to relocate his proper dimension based on his qualities and traits."

Joey grabbed onto me, and cradled me like I was one of his children ready to be put to bed. He reached towards my foot, the real one, grasped a tuft of fur, and yanked it right out of the follicles. I barely noticed this, however, because of the state of confusion and loss of feeling to most parts of my body.

"Fur from the feet should give us more luck," he said with a grin forming on his face. We entered the dimension machine as my father finished the setup processes. "Here's the fur Mr. Fuzzies. I hope it's enough to get the coordinates from because I don't know how much longer he'll last staying here…"

"Goodness, golly, gosh! He's fading even more than before!" Dad inserted the sample into the foreign object scanner, and extracted the coordinates approximate to where we would be in our dimension at this moment in time. "There, now just push the main button on the console, and get back to your home!" he said as he hastily exited the vehicle. "And son, I love you!" That was the last thing I heard my father say…

Blackness, the void had nearly consumed me. I awakened to the pitch blackness of a seemingly endless room. A spotlight shined from far above, down onto what could be the floor to this place, obsidian-like floors, with potentially razor sharp blades looming beneath the surface to impale those who weren't welcome here. A booming voice of ultimate power and wisdom filled the room. "BILLFORD FUZZIES!" I turned towards the source of this sound to find a pedestal, raised in darkness and light within the same material. I spotted a leg of some sort, strong and sinuous, brimming with muscle and power of a different kind. I followed the appendage upward, and spied the origin of this commanding voice. The only word that can describe this—thing—Godlike.

"I am the overlord of all dimensions, creator of space and time itself, destroyer of evil, the great God known as Oberiin. You have crossed the dimensions in a way never deemed fit! You have broken one of the sacred laws of the universe and time itself! What say you?"

I stared at this monstrous being of none, and all species at once, human, rabbit, eagle, dolph—

"SPEAK I SAY!!" I stumbled to the floor and tried to regain my composure. I was currently meeting with a Godly creature. Do as he said or risk being killed in whatever fashion suits his current mood!

"I meant not what I have done! It was all an accident!" I stated.

"This pathetic excuse does NOT amuse me! I have been lenient towards your kind until now, letting you traverse time itself, knowing the risk to the time continuum! NOW, SOMEONE MUST BE PUNISHED! You have nearly broken the dimensional boundaries between your dimension and the one you just attempted to flee! This cannot stand! And that infernal machine, the interdimensional travel machine, it threatens to destroy ALL of the boundaries set up by me and my forefathers at the beginning of time! Would you have me just let it ALL be destroyed for the sake of one lesser being allowed to live?"

I cowered and prostrated myself upon the ground in fear of what would happen if I angered this being any more than I already had. "Oh great being! I beg for forgiveness. It was an accident! The black hole sucked us in while I was time traveling. There was nothing I could do!"

"Dare you blame me for such folly? YOU had known that there could have been many catastrophic outcomes from the course of action that you took. Yet, you did it anyway!"

How could I convince this other worldly power that this was all a mistake and that I wished just to go home and return to my average life as a trillionaire playbunny? I couldn't buy my way out of this one (Gods like him couldn't be bought with the same money he literally created). As he prepared to lay his final judgement onto my soul, a plan sprung into my mind. It would be my only chance at survival.

"For you to annihilate me would mean nothing! The world would have learned nothing of the dangers of interdimensional travel and meddling with the time continuum. If you slaughter me here and now, there will be no lesson for the people to learn from. No example of what not to do."

"And what is it that makes you think that I should just let you live after the near universal destruction that you could have caused?" He stared at me with an inquisitive look of curiosity and intrigue.

"I suggest to you, that I be made into an example. One to the people of the universe to not test the almighty ones such as yourself. Oberiin, punish me how you see fit. Just let me live and return to my dimension with my friend, Joey, to live out my remaining years as an example."

"Even if I wanted to, there is but one issue with what you suggest. Joey is not of your dimension. He is a figment of your schizophrenic hare mind." This realization hit me like an asteroid hitting a planet.

"But if Joey—" I didn't get far into my argument before I was interrupted. "That is your punishment. Since you seem to care for your friend, Joey, and seeing as how he never existed in the first place, I shall do you a service and cure your schizophrenia, thus crushing Joey out of existence in your mind and the minds of anyone you had ever convinced of his existence."

"NO!! Joey is my only friend. He has been there for me through thick and thin. I CANNOT LET HIM DIE, EVEN IF HE ISN'T REAL!!"

I started feeling a fury wash over me, and tried to get close enough to make him physically understand. But before I could get close, he waved his hand and froze my body in place.

"I would be thanking me if I were you. I am curing your disease. And in return all I wish from you is that you stop production of any time travel devices made by your father or any other of your kind, and prevent interdimensional travel from existing at all. Now begone with you! Return to your world and spread word of my generosity." He waved his hand a second time, and my vision faded to white, causing me to faint.

When my vision faded back into the real world, my world, I sat up and said, "Where am I?... When am I?" I took a gander about my surroundings and found that I was in a small clearing in what must have been a sprawling forest teeming with birds of various species. Their colored wings and tails blowing calmly in the breeze. The quiet sounds of the forest, chirping of birds, rustling of tree leaves in the wind, and the distant sound of what could be a... factory?

I rose from my seemingly drunken stupor, and wandered the forest, only to find that this was no forest, not entirely anyway. This was a park in the center of some large city. I roamed the grounds until I located an exit, then went to the nearest shop window big enough to see my reflection in.

As I gazed partially into the window, I saw the same rabbit figure that I had seen my entire life. My fur its average brownish tint, with small white specks here and there. My clothes, although a bit shaggy, were my normal attire of a fitted suit matching the color of my fur, dusty and in dire need of a dry cleaning. Overall my image seemed a bit ragged and worn, but I was still intact.

Than I remembered why I was back, to stop the spread of time and interdimensional travel. And my punishment for having tampered with it... losing Joey. Although my mind felt perfectly stable for the first time since childhood, I couldn't help but miss my aetherial friend. I turned my face towards the cracked and aged sidewalk, and began to sob at my loss until a random passerby walked up and put his paw on my shoulder and said, "Hey! Is something wrong little fella?"

I looked over my shoulder to see a rather tall hare, staring at me with a look of concern and sympathy. I looked away again, and gave the obvious answer. "Yes, something is wrong."

"Why are you crying little bunny?"

"I am a grown rabbit, and won't be called a bunny. If you wish to address me, my name is Billford Fuzzies." Why wouldn't this lumbering buffoon just leave me alone?

"Well Billford, what's wrong?"

Clearly he wouldn't leave until he had found out the reason for my distress. So I told him. "I've lost the only friend that I'll probably ever have, and my only task in life now is to prevent my family from being successful. I've been doomed to destroy my family legacy. My life is falling into an endless pit, and I don't know if I'll ever get out of it."

He leaned in closer, and told me something that I doubt I shall ever forget. "Well, that's where you could be wrong Billford. If you spend your entire life looking down into the abyss, you might not notice that the top is just an arm's reach above you."

I turned around, wiping the few remaining tears from my face and asked, "Who are you?"

He smiled and said, "Me? My name is Jimmy Dinks. Nice to meet you Billford."

And that is where I met my first real friend with whom to have truly grand adventures with. Joey may not be here anymore, but I shall always remember him as my first true friend. I will never forget his memory.

SIGMA'S BOOKSHELF

Sigma's Bookshelf (www.SigmasBookshelf.com) is an independent book publishing company that exclusively publishes the work of teenage authors, who are between the ages of 12 - 19. The company was founded in 2016 by Minnesota teenager Justin M. Anderson, whose first book, *Saving Stripes: A Kitty's Story*, was published when he was 14, and has since sold hundreds of copies.

"I know there are a lot of other teenagers out there who are good writers and deserve to have their work published, but don't have access to the kinds of resources I do. I wanted to help them," he said.

Sigma's Bookshelf is a sponsored project of Springboard for the Arts, a nonprofit arts service organization. Contributions on behalf of Sigma's Bookshelf may be made payable to Springboard for the Arts and are tax deductible to the extent permitted by law. Donations can be made online at www.SigmasBookshelf.com/donate.

www.ingramcontent.com/pod-product-compliance
Lightning Source LLC
Chambersburg PA
CBHW021027120726
47905CB00009B/3219